OUR POLICE

written & illustrated by
Jack E. Levin

with a preface by his son

Mark R. Levin

OUR POLICE

POLICE

aladdin

NEW YORK   LONDON   TORONTO   SYDNEY   NEW DELHI

ALADDIN | An imprint of Simon & Schuster Children's Publishing Division | 1230 Avenue of the Americas, New York, New York 10020 | First Aladdin hardcover edition October 2018 | Copyright © 2018 by Jack E. Levin | Preface copyright © 2018 by Mark R. Levin | All rights reserved, including the right of reproduction in whole or in part in any form. | ALADDIN and related logo are registered trademarks of Simon & Schuster, Inc. | For information about special discounts for bulk purchases, please contact Simon & Schuster Special Sales at 1-866-506-1949 or business@simonandschuster.com. | The Simon & Schuster Speakers Bureau can bring authors to your live event. For more information or to book an event contact the Simon & Schuster Speakers Bureau at 1-866-248-3049 or visit our website at www.simonspeakers.com. | Book designed by Karin Paprocki | The illustrations for this book were rendered in marker and gouache. | The text of this book was set in Adorn Slab Serif Regular. | Manufactured in China 0818 SCP | 2 4 6 8 10 9 7 5 3 1 | Library of Congress Control Number 2018936498 | ISBN 978-1-5344-2950-5 (hc) | ISBN 978-1-5344-2951-2 (eBook)

This book was created for
young people, with the HOPE that
it will HELP them look upon the police
as friends, guardians, and protectors
who work hard and tirelessly to keep
our world SAFE and SECURE.

PREFACE BY MARK R. LEVIN

GROWING UP AS A YOUNG CHILD and then teenager on the tough streets of Philadelphia in the 1920s and 1930s, my father, Jack, gained a fond appreciation for the role of the police. My parents taught us from a young age to respect the police and their difficult job. In fact, two of my uncles served in the Philadelphia police department. Uncle Willie was a motorcycle officer and Uncle Jack was a traffic officer.

My father is a deeply patriotic man with a great deal of common sense. He understands that in all walks of life, and in every profession, man's imperfections present themselves. But having witnessed recent events and related news reports painting police officers and police departments in an extremely negative light, he felt a book especially geared to our young people was essential so that they learn to respect law and order.

If you could imagine an America without law and order, it would be a place where people would be free to create all kinds of trouble, endangering our lives, families, businesses, and lifestyles. In other words, America would cease being the America we know and love, a civil society where the "life, liberty, and happiness" of the individual are cherished and protected.

While our government is established with various institutions that have as their purpose the preservation of our "unalienable rights," it is left to law enforcement, particularly our community and neighborhood police officers, to ensure that our lives, property, and everyday activities are safeguarded. Police officers are also on the front lines as the first responders when the public is threatened by acts of nature such as earthquakes or hurricanes, or by acts of man that endanger the public safety. In certain instances our police officers serve as neutral protectors of our rights as citizens, such as guaranteeing the safety of peaceful protesters who may march down a public street chanting slogans we might find offensive. For these reasons, police officers are often referred to as "peace officers."

My father is now ninety-three years old. He has authored and illustrated several wonderful children's books. In each book he seeks to open the eyes and minds of young people to the greatness of American history, principles, and values. He wants the next generation to be as proud of America as his generation. In *Our Police*, my father has written and illustrated another beautiful book. From my family to yours, we hope you enjoy it!

· POLICE ·

Police officers are persons charged with the enforcement of the laws of a community. They must study and work very hard, completing written exams and physical tests to become officers of the law.

Those who wear the blue and the badge of the police all share one thing in common: they put their lives on the line to protect and serve all the people of their communities. They never know what lies ahead for them when reporting for duty—good, bad, or dangerous.

The

TRAFFIC POLICE

help children cross the street

safely on their way to school.

They keep cars,
buses, trucks, and
motorcycles—and all
the other vehicles
that make up traffic—
moving safely on our
very busy streets.

POLICE DOG HANDLERS

have very special partners: canines (K-9s). They train together and live together, and the canine is trained to perform certain tasks, like sniffing out evidence or locating suspects.

The most popular police dog breeds include German shepherd, Belgian Malinois, and Dutch shepherd.

Horses are also members of some departments.

MOUNTED
POLICE OFFICERS

control crowds of people by

bravely riding into the middle

of a group, quieting them down, and sending them on their way. It is all done with the help of their noble equine companions.

PATROL CAR OFFICERS

drive their cars in various neighborhoods,

continually making sure all is quiet

and peaceful. These police

are prepared to respond to anything—
including lost pets, stolen goods, and even
storms, floods, and anything that may
put people in danger. The cars, which
often have flashing lights and sirens,
help them quickly get to the scene.

If police officers get to the scene
of an accident first, they check to see if
anyone is hurt. Since they are trained
in first aid techniques, they attend to
any victims and try to make them as
comfortable as possible until an ambulance
arrives and takes them to the hospital.

When it comes to tough jobs, look toward the STATE TROOPERS. Those who ride motorcycles face all kinds of weather conditions—torrential rain, blinding snow, winter cold, and summer heat—doing their best to help drivers in need and making sure they follow state laws and regulations.

Sometimes they chase speeding cars or reckless drivers and have to approach the vehicle carefully when pulling someone over to issue a ticket.

Ahoy to the

WATER POLICE,

a special force that patrols the
waterways and keeps boats, ships,
and even kayaks safe from harm.

Yes, water police do save lives, rescuing people from boats that have sunk or capsized, those who fall overboard and can't swim,

and swimmers who venture out too
far and can't make it back to shore.

When a fierce hurricane hits, the police remain steadfast. Amid the rising floodwaters, they search for missing people and stranded pets.

Everyone is exhausted, hungry, and soaked.

But that's not all. . . .

The police search the flooded area once the hurricane has passed. They find and rescue people stranded on the roofs of their homes or cars.

Here, a police officer assists a stranded woman and her young child, helping hold her baby until they get into the rescue boat.

SEARCH AND RESCUE

The police don't just serve on land or on water. They also watch over us from the sky.

POLICE

POLICE HELICOPTER PILOTS

can quickly transport sick people

to hospitals, and because they can

see miles in any direction, they

can provide security at major events.

One of the main jobs of the police helicopter pilot is to fly at night, shining the powerful light on the nose of the helicopter down onto the ground to make sure all is safe in the surrounding neighborhood.

for the members of our great police force,

those here in America and those throughout

the world, who are steadfastly dedicated

and committed to our safety, security, and well-being. Yes, a great big HOORAY for our police.

To the people who are

TRUE
TO
THE BLUE.

We look up to them with

HONOR,
RESPECT,
ADMIRATION,

and

THANKS.